DRAGON MASTERS

SHINE OF THE SILVER DRAGON

BY

TRACEY WEST

SCHOLASTIC INC.

DRAGON MASTERS

Read All the Adventures

TABLE OF CONTENTS

TO MY FRIEND LARA,

who is as strong and smart and brave as Jean. — TW

Library of Congress Cataloging-in-Publication Data
Names: West, Tracey, 1965- author. De Polonia, Nina, illustrator. West, Tracey, 1965- Dragon Masters; 11.
Title: Shine of the silver dragon / by Tracey West; illustrated by Nina de Polonia.
Description: First edition. New York: Branches/Scholastic Inc., 2018. Series: Dragon masters; 11
Summary: Diego is under the spell of the wizard Maldred who wants to control the Naga, an enormous dragon that lives deep within the Earth, and plans to use the boy to steal the two keys necessary for that purpose; the first key is guarded by Argent, the silver dragon, and Jean his dragon master, so Drake, Bo, Carlos, and their dragons travel to Gallia to try to stop the theft and break the spell on Diego.
Identifiers: LCCN 2017045313 ISBN 9781338263657 (pbk : alk. paper)
ISBN 9781338263664 (hbk : alk. paper)
Subjects: LCSH: Dragons—Juvenile fiction. Magic—Juvenile fiction. Wizards—Juvenile fiction. Locks and keys—Juvenile fiction. Adventure stories. CYAC: Dragons—Fiction. Magic—Fiction. Wizards—Fiction. Locks and keys—Fiction. Adventure and adventurers—Fiction. LCGFT: Action and adventure fiction.
Classification: LCC PZ7.W51937 Sgs 2018 DDC 813.54 [Fic] —dc23 LC record available at https://lccn.loc.gov/2017045313

10 9 8 7 6 5 4 3 2 1 18 19 20 21 22

Printed in China 62

First edition, October 2018
Illustrated by Nina de Polonia
Edited by Katie Carella
Book design by Jessica Meltzer

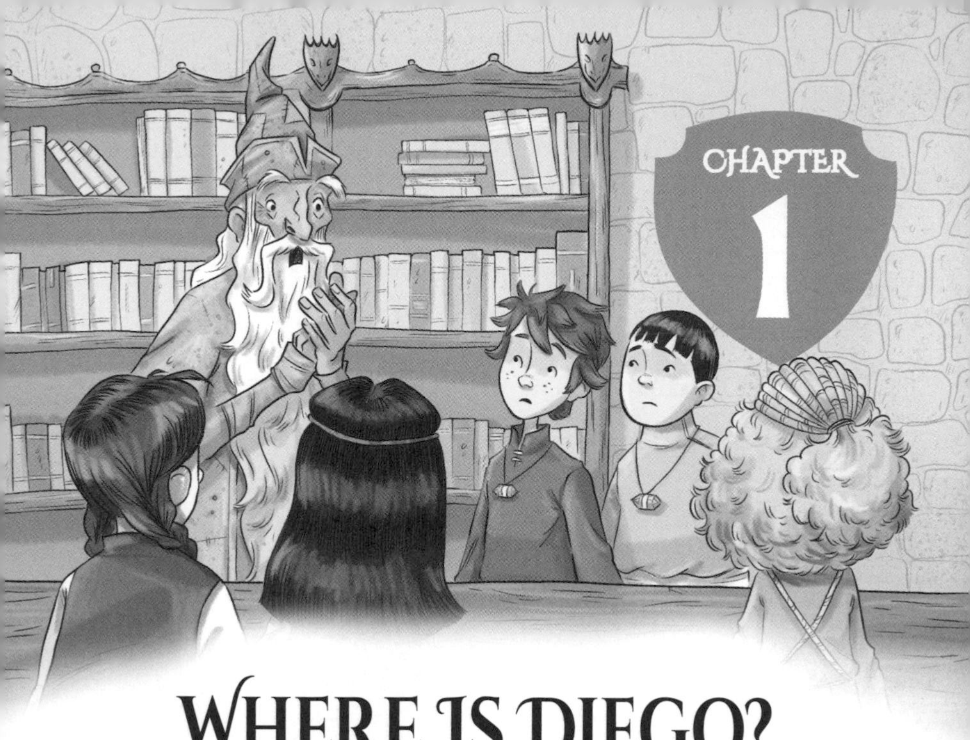

WHERE IS DIEGO?

Griffith the wizard clapped.

"Dragon Masters, settle down!" he said. "We have a lot to talk about."

Five Dragon Masters — Drake, Rori, Bo, Ana, and Petra — were gathered around the table in their classroom in King Roland's castle. Griffith, their teacher, had called them together for an important meeting.

Griffith cleared his throat, about to speak, when a boy rushed into the room.

"Carlos!" Drake cried. Carlos was another Dragon Master, who lived far away, in the Kingdom of Aragon.

"Something bad happened to Diego!" Carlos said. "Lalo and I flew here as fast as we could to tell you."

He pointed behind him, where a baby Lightning Dragon was shooting off sizzling sparks.

"I'm glad you're here," Griffith told him. "We know that Diego is in trouble. Please join us."

Carlos stood next to Ana.

Griffith cleared his throat again. "Now then, let's start at the beginning," he said. "Yesterday, I got word that Maldred had escaped from Wizard's Council prison."

"Who is Maldred?" Carlos asked.

"He is a bad wizard," Rori chimed in. "He attacked King Roland's castle once, but we defeated him."

She grabbed a book from a shelf. Then she flipped to a picture of Maldred. The wizard had a patch over one eye, and a long, pointy beard.

Carlos gasped. "That's him! That is the wizard who put a spell on Diego!"

"You saw him?" Griffith asked. "Please tell us what happened."

"Diego and I were eating in the kitchen. Diego has seashells on the wall that act as a magical alarm. They began to shake, so we knew dark magic was near," Carlos explained. "Diego told me to hide, and I did."

Petra gasped. "How scary!"

"I watched from my hiding place," Carlos said. "Maldred appeared out of nowhere. Diego tried to use magic against him, but it didn't work. Then Maldred said a spell, and Diego's eyes glazed over and turned red."

Drake got a chill. "The color of dark magic."

"Maldred vanished with Diego," Carlos said. "They were both gone before I could do anything."

"Diego poofed here," Bo said. "And he stole a book: *The Lore of the Ancient One*."

Drake had seen Diego "poof" many times before. Diego waved his wand and could transport anywhere in a flash.

"Why would Diego steal a book?" Carlos asked.

Ana frowned. "Griffith, you said the book was about something called the Naga, and that the whole world could be in danger. What did you mean by that?"

A dark look crossed Griffith's face. "I must tell you all a story," he said. "The tale of a legendary dragon known as the Naga."

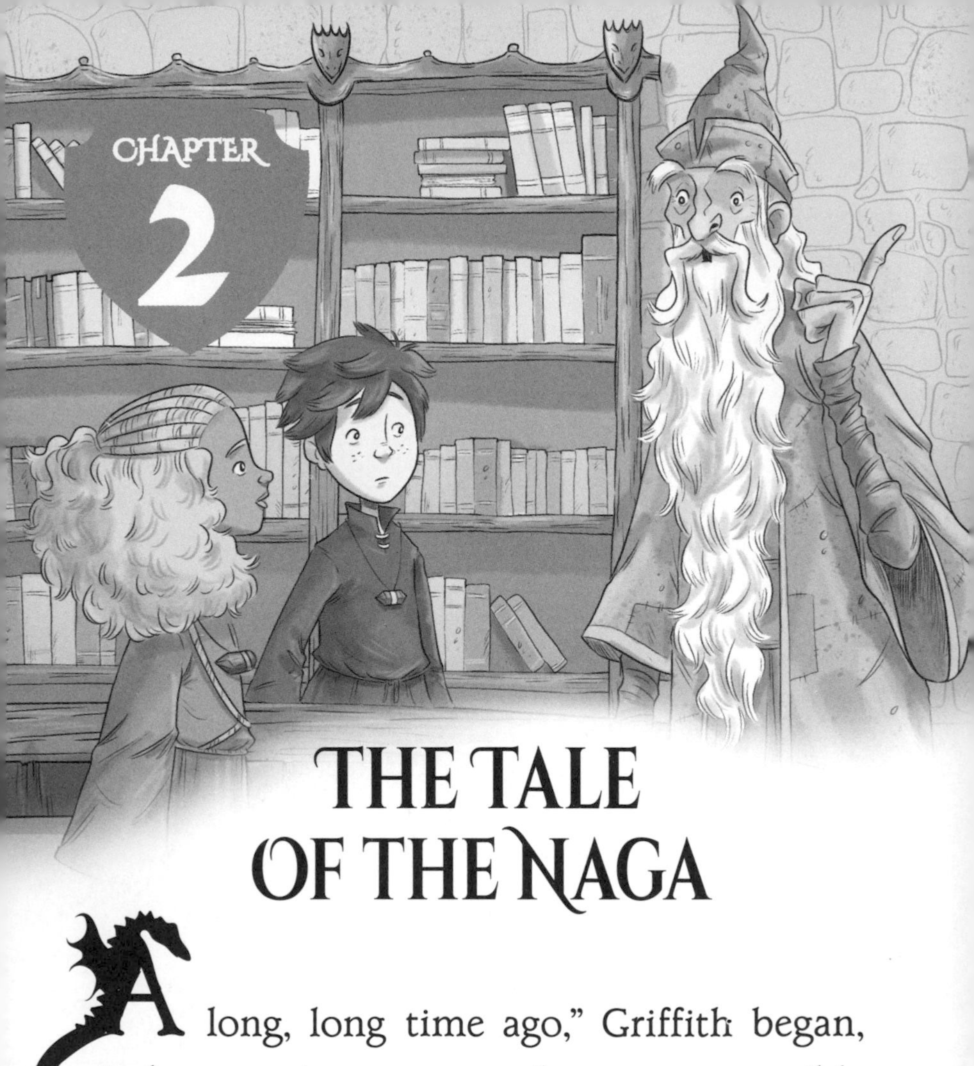

THE TALE OF THE NAGA

"A long, long time ago," Griffith began, "when magic was new, there was a terrible earthquake."

"I was in an earthquake once," Petra said. "The ground shook. And some buildings in my village crumbled into pieces."

"During this terrible earthquake, the ground opened up," Griffith continued. "It coughed up a dragon egg from the deepest part of the world. The egg was as big as a mountain."

Bo's eyes got wide. "Was that the Naga's egg?"

"Yes," Griffith replied. "The Naga has the power of earthquakes. He uses the power of his mind, much like Worm does." Griffith was talking about Drake's Earth Dragon, Worm.

"The Naga sounds much bigger than Worm," Drake said.

"Indeed," Griffith agreed. "And his power is one hundred times greater than Worm's."

Drake's mouth dropped open. He couldn't imagine Worm being that powerful!

Griffith went on. "When the young Naga hatched, he could not control his powers. He started to destroy the earth. He brought down mountains. He caused great floods."

"Oh no! That's terrible!" Ana cried. "Did anybody stop him?"

"Yes. The wizards did," Griffith answered. "They knew the Naga was too big, and too powerful, to be out in the world. So they returned him to his home."

"How did they do that?" Petra asked.

“They made two magical tools that gave them control of the Naga,” Griffith replied. “The wizards of the north made the Silver Key. And the wizards of the south made the Gold Key. They used these keys to make the Naga go back into the earth.”

Drake realized something. “When Maldred attacked the castle, he was trying to take Worm so he could use his powers,” he said. “Do you think he wants to use the Naga for his powers, too?”

“I am afraid so,” Griffith replied.

“Where are the keys now?” Petra asked.

Griffith held up his finger. Blue sparks shot from it. He began to draw an image in the air out of magical blue light.

The first image was a round disc with strange-looking symbols on it.

“This is the Silver Key,” Griffith said. “It is hidden somewhere in the northern part of the world, guarded by a Silver Dragon.”

He drew another disc, with different symbols.

"This is the Gold Key," he said. "It is hidden somewhere in the southern part of the world, guarded by a Gold Dragon."

"And the book Diego stole tells how to find the keys . . ." Drake guessed, and the wizard nodded.

Then Rori said aloud what they were all thinking: "If Maldred finds these keys, he will have control of the Naga. He could destroy the world!"

A NEW MISSION

The Dragon Masters followed Griffith to his workshop.

"We must find Diego before Maldred uses him to do another evil deed," Griffith said as they walked down the hall.

"There's something I don't understand," Carlos said. "Why didn't Maldred steal the book himself? Why did he need Diego to do it for him?"

"Maldred knows that Diego and I are friends, so he knew Diego could get into this castle easily," Griffith replied.

"We need to find Diego, before he finds the keys and gives them to Maldred," Petra said.

"Right!" Griffith agreed.

They entered the workshop. The room was piled high with strange things. Shelves held dozens of bottles filled with colorful waters and powders.

Griffith rushed to the magical gazing ball and placed his hand over it. The large glass globe lit up.

"Diego, Diego, where did you go?" Griffith asked, waving his hand over the ball.

Hazy smoke swirled inside the ball. They all waited quietly, watching. Then the haze cleared, and an image appeared. An image of a short, round wizard.

"Diego!" Carlos cried.

Diego was standing at the foot of a hill. On top of the hill sat a sturdy-looking stone castle.

"I know this castle," Griffith said. "It is in the Land of Gallia, not far from here."

"We are in the northern part of the world," Petra said. "So maybe the Silver Key is in Gallia!"

Griffith stroked his beard. "That is a good guess. I studied *The Lore of the Ancient One* for many years. But even I could not learn the exact location of the keys. The book is written in an ancient magical language."

"Can Maldred read the ancient magical language?" Ana asked.

"Better than I can," Griffith replied. "So if Diego is in Gallia, then the key must be there."

He pointed at Drake, Bo, and Carlos. "You three must get to Gallia right away," he said.

Rori folded her arms across her chest. "Why do only the boys get to go?"

"We have a long fight ahead of us. I must choose Dragon Masters carefully for each mission," Griffith explained. "Carlos knows Diego best, so he and Lalo must go. A Water Dragon's powers should be able to cure Diego of the dark spell, so Bo and Shu must go. And Drake and Worm can transport everyone there quickly."

"I guess that makes sense," Rori replied, frowning. "But I'm definitely going on the next mission!"

"I know I can always count on you, Rori," Griffith said. "Now, Drake and Bo, go to the Dragon Caves and leave from there. Carlos and Lalo will follow you."

"Good luck!" Ana said.

Drake waved to Ana, Rori, and Petra. "We won't let you down."

"Hurry!" Griffith said. "You must stop Diego from getting the Silver Key!"

CHAPTER 4

THE CASTLE

A few minutes later, Drake, Carlos, and Bo stood outside the Dragon Caves with their dragons.

Bo's dragon, Shu, was a blue Water Dragon. She had no wings but was able to fly on air currents. She floated over to Bo's side like a ship sailing on the waves.

Lalo the baby Lightning Dragon was half the size of Shu. The yellow dragon constantly sparked with electric energy. Since he was still a young dragon, he did not have full control of his powers yet.

"Calm down, Lalo," Carlos told him. "We will find Diego."

Drake's Earth Dragon, Worm, had a long, brown body and two tiny wings. He couldn't fly, but he could transport anywhere in the world in a flash.

Drake looked down at the green Dragon Stone he wore around his neck. All Dragon Masters wore one just like it. His stone was glowing green, which meant that he and Worm had a strong connection.

Drake, Carlos, and Bo all touched Worm. Bo touched Shu, and Carlos put one hand on Lalo.

"Worm, take us to Gallia — to the castle we saw in the gazing ball!" Drake said.

Worm's body glowed green. The light exploded. Drake closed his eyes to shield them from the brightness.

When he opened his eyes, all three Dragon Masters and their dragons were at the bottom of a hill.

Drake gazed up at the gray stone castle they had seen in the gazing ball. The center of the castle – called the keep – was one big, three-story rectangle. Four round, three-story towers surrounded the keep.

"Do you think Diego is already inside?" Bo asked.

"He might be," Drake replied.

Carlos stared up at the castle, and he bit his lower lip. "There must be a lot of soldiers guarding the key," he said. "What if they have captured Diego?"

"Then we'll rescue him," Drake said.

"We need to get inside quick," Bo said. "Should Worm transport us there?"

"No one knows we're here yet," Drake replied. "If Worm transports us into the castle, his bright light might give us away. Let's walk around the hill and sneak up from behind."

"I'll try to keep Lalo calm, so his sparks don't give us away, either," Carlos offered.

They walked around the hill and then climbed up to the castle. The land was eerily quiet. Drake kept his eyes on the four towers but didn't see any soldiers.

"I think Shu and I should fly up to that tower," Bo said, pointing. "If there are soldiers up there, we'll catch them by surprise."

Drake nodded. "And then Worm and I can transport. If we do it fast enough, we can get ahead of the soldiers before they —"

Whoosh!

Something whizzed past Drake's ear. He jumped to the side as he realized what it was: a rock. More rocks the size of apples came shooting down from the top of the tower.

"We're being attacked!" Carlos yelled.

UNDER ATTACK!

"Worm, protect us!" Drake commanded.

Worm's body glowed green, and the rocks froze in midair. Then they all harmlessly dropped straight down to the ground.

"What should we do?" Bo asked.

"Lalo could fly up there and zap the soldiers so they will stop throwing rocks," Carlos suggested.

Bo shook his head. “We don’t want to attack the people guarding this castle,” he said. “They are just trying to protect the key. We need to let them know we are here to help them.”

Drake frowned. “There must be a whole army up there!”

Then his Dragon Stone glowed green, and he heard Worm’s voice in his head.

Just one.

“Just one?” Drake asked. “One what? One army?”

One soldier.

“One soldier?” Drake repeated.

“That’s impossible!” Carlos cried. Another wave of rocks showered down from the tower, and Worm quickly stopped them in midair.

“One person couldn’t be throwing all of these rocks!” Bo agreed.

"Worm is always right about these things," Drake said. He looked at his dragon. "What should we do, Worm?"

Transport to the tower.

Drake touched Worm and turned to Carlos and Bo. "Worm wants us all to transport up to the tower," he said.

"I trust Worm," Bo said, and he touched Worm's tail.

"I do, too," Carlos added, following Bo's lead.

Worm transported them in a flash, and they landed on top of the big, round tower.

As the green light faded, Worm saw a soldier marching toward them – a girl who looked to be eight years old, just like Drake and the others. She wore metal armor and carried a sword – a sword pointed right at Drake.

"Halt!" she yelled. "You may not enter this castle!"

CHAPTER 6

GUARDIAN OF THE SILVER KEY

"Stop!" Drake cried. He held up his hands to show he meant no harm. "We are not here to steal the Silver Key. We are here to help you protect it!"

The girl stopped marching toward them. But she did not lower her sword. "What do you know of the Silver Key?" she asked.

Drake had already noticed two important things about the girl: She did not seem to be afraid of their dragons, even though Lalo was nervously shooting off sparks behind Carlos. Also, she wore a green Dragon Stone around her neck.

"We are Dragon Masters, just like you," Drake said. He held up his own Dragon Stone to show her.

"I can see that," the girl said. "That does not mean I can trust you. I cannot let anyone enter this castle. It is my job to protect the key!"

"But we want to help you," Bo said. "A very bad wizard is trying to steal the key. We came here to stop him."

"You could be saying that to trick me," the girl said.

"We wouldn't do that," Drake said. "Our dragons are not attacking you right now, are they? And we know you're the only person in this castle."

The girl's dark eyes flashed. "How do you know that?"

Drake pointed to Worm. "My Earth Dragon, Worm, has some pretty awesome mind powers," he said. "I'm Drake, by the way. This is Bo and his dragon, Shu. And that's Carlos and his dragon, Lalo."

The girl lowered her sword. "I'm Jean," she said. "And you may be telling the truth. But you still cannot enter this castle."

Drake was about to speak when he noticed something strange. Worm had closed his eyes, and his body was softly glowing.

"What's happening, Worm?" Drake asked.

I am reaching out to Jean's dragon, the Earth Dragon replied.

Suddenly, Jean's Dragon Stone began to glow. Drake knew she was hearing her dragon's voice inside her head. Her eyes widened in surprise.

"Argent says that I must let you in," she said. "I will do what he wishes."

"Is Argent your dragon?" Bo asked.

"Yes," she said, waving for them all to follow her. "Come."

"Where are we going?" Drake asked.

Jean smiled for the first time. "To the lair of the Silver Dragon," she replied.

JEAN'S STORY

They started to follow Jean across the tower, but Carlos stopped.

"I think Lalo and I should stay here," he said. "I can keep him calm, and we can keep a lookout for Diego."

"Is Diego this very bad wizard you spoke of?" Jean asked.

"No," Drake replied. "But the very bad wizard, Maldred, has put Diego under a spell. He sent Diego here to steal the Silver Key."

"Then we must not let him get inside the castle," Jean said. "Carlos, let me show you something."

She walked to the edge of the tower, looking out over the hillside. A dozen catapults were lined up along the tower's edge.

"These don't look like any of the catapults I have seen before," Carlos said.

A catapult usually had a heavy weight on one end and a basket holding a large rock on the other. But at the end of each of these catapults was a long, narrow basket with ten rocks nestled inside.

"I improved them," Jean explained. "When you cut the rope attached to the basket, the weight will drop. Then the rocks will go flying forward. I changed these catapults to shoot several rocks so it looks like there are many soldiers up here."

Wow! Jean is really smart! Drake thought.

"Your idea worked," he said. "We thought we were facing an army!"

Jean smiled and then turned to Carlos. "I've got six more catapults loaded, if you need them," she told him.

Then she walked over to the opposite wall, where a rope was hanging. "Pull on this rope if you see any wizards. A bell will ring in Argent's lair."

Carlos nodded. "I will!"

Jean knelt down and opened a door on the floor. Drake, Bo, and their dragons followed her down a long, twisting stairway.

"Do you live here all alone?" Drake asked.

"I am not alone," Jean replied. "Argent is here with me."

"Don't you have a wizard?" Bo asked.

"The wizard lives with the king of Gallia, far from here," Jean explained. "Nobody can be trusted to guard the Silver Key except Argent and his Dragon Master. Argent has been guarding the key since the wizards of the north first made it."

"Griffith, our wizard, told us that the keys were made a very long time ago," Drake said. "So Argent must have had many Dragon Masters."

"Yes," Jean said. "I am proud to be his newest master."

"Don't you get lonely?" Bo asked.

They had come to a door at the end of the staircase.

"I keep myself busy," Jean said. She opened the door. "Come, I will show you."

AWESOME INVENTIONS

Drake, Bo, and their dragons followed Jean into a big room filled with all kinds of strange-looking objects made out of metal, gears, and wires. Some looked like weapons, and others looked like toys. Drake stopped in front of a metal bird sitting on top of a wooden post.

“Turn the handle,” Jean said, pointing to a curved bar coming out of the post. Drake thought he saw a twinkle in her eye.

He turned the handle, and the bird began to spin around in a circle.

“Cool!” Drake cried.

“Did you make all of this stuff?” Bo asked.

Jean shrugged. “It helps to pass the time.”

“I have never known anybody who could make such awesome inventions,” Drake said.

Jean looked pleased for a second, but then her face grew serious. "That is enough talk about my inventions. Tell me about this evil wizard, Maldred."

"Maldred just escaped from Wizard's Council prison," Drake said. "We think he wants to steal the silver and gold keys so that he can control the Naga and destroy the world."

"We don't know where he is," Bo added. "But we know that Diego is under his spell. Luckily, my dragon, Shu, can wash dark spells away. He will cure Diego."

"But it won't be easy. Diego has a special magic that lets him poof in and out of places," Drake explained. "We have to act fast when we see him, so he doesn't poof away with the Silver Key before Shu can cure him."

Jean smiled. "He cannot poof into Argent's lair," she said. "It is protected by powerful magic."

"Maybe," Drake said. "But Maldred has broken through magical barriers before. If he is adding his power to Diego's, Diego might be able to get into the lair."

"We will see," she said.

She led Drake, Bo, Worm, and Shu into a long hallway. They followed her to a big door. Jean spun a series of gears that clicked and whirred until the door opened. Drake was surprised to see a second door behind it.

Jean spun more gears and opened the second door, which revealed one more door.

Argent's lair is really well protected! Drake thought.

Jean pushed open the third door.

A bright silver glare hit Drake's eyes

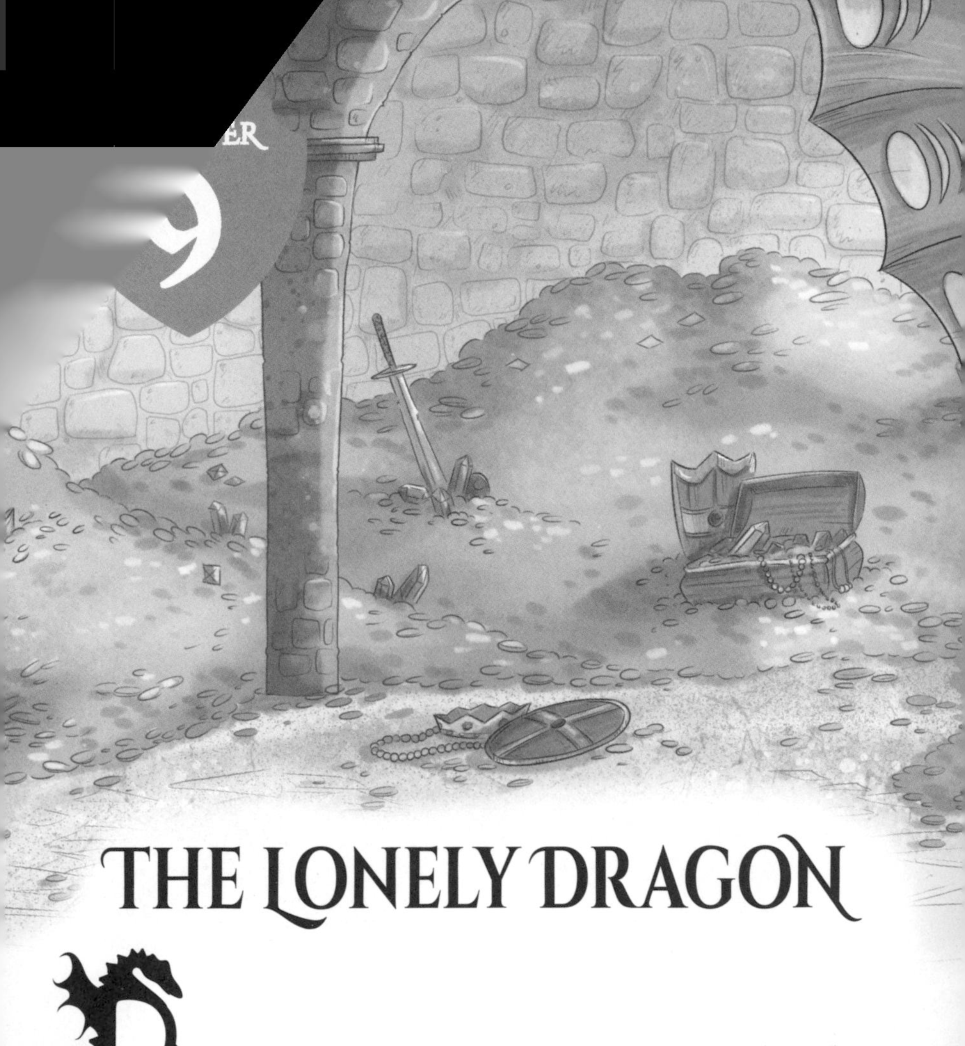

CHAPTER 9

THE LONELY DRAGON

Drake shielded his eyes. *Is that bright shine coming from a dragon?* he thought.

"Argent, stand down!" Jean commanded. "These are the Dragon Masters that you told me to let in."

The silver shine faded, revealing the most beautiful dragon Drake had ever seen. The dragon's body was covered in shimmering silver scales. The design on his large wings reminded Drake of a butterfly's wings, but all in silver.

"Argent shines when he thinks danger is near," Jean explained.

Drake's Dragon Stone began to glow. He heard Worm's voice in his head.

I communicated with Argent when we were on the tower. I think he trusts me. But Argent will attack if he thinks we will steal the key.

Drake looked at Argent. "Don't worry," he told Jean's dragon. "We are here to protect the key, not steal it."

He and Bo gazed around the dragon's lair. The big underground room had walls made of stone. Torches on the walls lit up the darkness. They cast a glow on a mound of silver treasures: goblets, coins, swords, and jewelry.

"Wow!" Drake exclaimed. "This is a lot of treasure."

"These treasures are not important," Jean replied. "They are only here to confuse thieves. The Silver Key is hidden in this lair."

As she spoke, Argent began moving across the floor toward the other dragons. His blue eyes gazed at Worm and Shu. Then he moved even closer, looking directly into Worm's eyes.

"Argent has never seen another dragon before," Jean said.

Bo gently touched the Silver Dragon's tail. "That is sad," he said. "Our dragons all have one another."

“Argent knows that guarding the Silver Key is a great honor, just as I do,” Jean said. Then she smiled a little. “Still, it is nice to have company.”

Shu opened her mouth and a watery mist floated out.

Bo laughed. “I think Shu is showing off for Argent,” he said.

"Argent must have incredible powers," Drake said. "What can he do?"

Jean smiled again. "Argent can blast his enemies with his silver shine," she replied. "And when his opponent attacks, his wings reflect the attack right back at them."

Drake's mouth dropped open. "That is an amazing power!"

Suddenly, a bell rang in the lair.

"Carlos!" Jean cried. "He must have spotted one of the wizards!"

GET READY!

Argent's body began to shine brightly.

Jean drew her sword.

The air sizzled with magical energy.

Drake felt his skin prickle. "Worm, what's happening?"

Worm closed his eyes, and his body began to glow.

Diego is trying to break through the magical barrier.

"Diego is trying to get in!" Drake told the others.

"We must protect the Silver Key!" Jean cried.

"Right," Drake said. "Bo, if Diego gets into the lair, command Shu to blast him with her healing mist."

Bo patted his dragon. "Get ready, Shu!"

Then Drake heard Worm's voice again.

Maldred has added his power to Diego's. Diego is very strong now. Strong enough to break into the lair.

It was just what Drake had feared. But Drake didn't repeat Worm's words. He didn't want to upset Bo or Jean. There had to be a way to protect the key . . .

He whirled around to Jean.

"If Diego gets in, Worm could transport the key out of here to somewhere safe. Just like he transported us onto the tower before," he said. "Where is the key?"

Jean frowned. "I cannot tell you," she said. "How can I be sure that Worm will bring the key back here?"

"Jean, please! Trust us!" Drake begged. "Worm can transport it out of here, Shu can cure Diego, and then I promise we'll bring the key right back to you."

Jean looked at Argent. "What should we do?" she asked her dragon.

Suddenly, Argent let out a piercing shriek. He started to flap his wings. Then . . .

BOOM!

A loud explosion rocked the dragon's lair.

DIEGO VS. THE DRAGONS

Diego appeared in a swirling cloud of red smoke. Red energy glowed from his body. His red-glazed eyes looked wild.

Drake waited for Bo to command Shu, but his friend was silent. Bo was frozen with shock at seeing Diego looking so evil.

"Bo, Shu needs to cure Diego now!" Drake yelled.

But Bo stayed silent, and Diego pointed at Shu. The Water Dragon looked at Bo, confused. Drake knew that Shu wouldn't attack Diego, a friend, unless Bo told her to.

Red magic sparked from Diego's fingertips. He hit Shu with a big blast of dark energy, knocking her out.

Bo shook off his fear. "Shu!" he cried, kneeling at her side.

"Worm, freeze Diego!" Drake yelled.

Worm's body glowed. Bright green light surrounded Diego, but the wizard walked right through it.

"Argent, attack!" Jean yelled.

"No!" Drake cried.

Argent's silver shine got even brighter.

He roared, and a bright beam of light shot from his mouth, aimed at Diego.

Diego held up both hands. Red magic flowed out of his fingertips and he waved his arms, pushing the blast aside. Argent's silver energy exploded in a pile of treasure.

Then the wizard shot a blast of red energy right at Argent. The Silver Dragon held up a shining wing. The red magic bounced off the wing and hit Diego!

The wizard went flying backward and banged his head on a silver chest. His eyes closed, and his head drooped to one side.

Drake turned to Jean. "Please don't let Argent hurt Diego anymore," he said. "We can still cure him."

"I must protect the key, at all costs," Jean replied.

Drake glanced over at Shu. The Water Dragon was stirring. In just a minute, she'd be able to heal Diego. But Shu would need time to break the spell that Maldred had put on Diego.

Drake knew that Argent would attack as soon as Jean commanded him to. He couldn't let that happen.

"Worm, freeze Argent!" Drake yelled.

Worm began to glow.

Jean's eyes narrowed. She pointed her sword at Drake's chest.

"No," she said firmly. "Stop Worm right now!"

ARGENT'S POWERS

Worm's body started to glow brighter. Jean took a step closer to Drake.

Drake looked right into Jean's eyes. "You wouldn't hurt me," he said.

"I do not want to," Jean said. "But I am sworn to protect the key. I cannot fail." She did not lower her sword.

"Please, Jean. Just give Shu a chance to heal Diego," Drake said.

"What if it doesn't work? I cannot take any chances," she replied. "Call off Worm!"

"I'm sorry, Jean. But I cannot take any chances either," Drake said. He turned to Worm. "Freeze Argent now!"

With a roar, Worm shot a blast of green energy at Argent.

The Silver Dragon reflected it with his shining wing, but Worm was expecting that. He quickly transported out of the way.

Next, Worm aimed a blast at Argent's tail, but the Silver Dragon whipped around and blocked it with his other wing.

Worm, find some way to stop Argent! Drake pleaded inside his mind.

"I said, call him off!" Jean repeated.

Suddenly, her sword clattered to the ground. She spun around to see Bo standing behind her. He had knocked the sword from her hands using a piece of treasure!

"I can't let you hurt Drake," Bo told her.

Bo and Jean stared at each other. Argent's silver shine became almost blinding as he got ready to attack Worm with a powerful energy blast.

"Worm, watch out!" Drake cried. Then he felt a prickle on the back of his neck. Drake quickly turned around. Diego was awake!

The wizard floated across the lair! His body glowed with red energy once more. The red light sparkled across the silver riches below.

"Jean! Bo! Look!" Drake yelled.

Diego pointed at the treasure pile. The goblets, coins, and jewels shook. Then a sparkling silver disc rose up from within the pile. It floated right into Diego's hand.

"It's the Silver Key!" Jean cried. "Argent, attack the wizard!"

A WIN AND A LOSS

Argent turned toward Diego. But before he could blast the wizard, Bo yelled out a command: "Shu, heal Diego!"

Shu rushed over to the wizard. A blue cloud of water flowed from Shu's mouth. A light blue mist rained down on him.

Diego stopped moving.

The red glow faded from his body. Soon he looked just like the Diego that the Dragon Masters knew.

"He's cured!" Bo cried.

"Argent, stand down!" Jean cried, and the Silver Dragon's shine faded.

Diego blinked. "Drake? Bo? Where am I?" he asked.

"You're in Gallia, in the lair of the Silver Dragon," Drake replied. "Maldred had put a spell on you. You were under his control."

Diego gazed down at the sparkly silver disc in his hand. "Oh no . . ." he said. "Did Maldred want me to steal this key?"

"You were about to bring it to him! But Shu healed you just in time," Bo told him.

"The last thing I remember, Carlos and I were in my cottage, and I told him to hide from Maldred," Diego said. "Is Carlos okay?"

"He is on the tower with Lalo," Drake said. "He rang a bell to warn us that you were coming."

Now Diego noticed Jean. "I am very sorry that I tried to steal the key," Diego said to her.

"And I'm sorry that Argent attacked you," Jean said. "And that I almost attacked you too, Drake. But we have to protect the key, no matter what."

Diego nodded. "I understand," he said. "This key is very important."

"Yes, it is," Jean said, "which is why it must stay here."

Diego held out the Silver Key. But before Jean could take it, a red orb appeared next to them.

Drake gasped. *That is one of Maldred's orbs!* He remembered seeing them before, in King Roland's castle and in Emperor Song's palace.

The orb zoomed down and absorbed the key right out of Diego's hands!

Argent roared and lunged at the orb. But the orb disappeared in a flash — and took the Silver Key with it!

DON'T GIVE UP!

"Maldred has the key," Drake said, and his face turned pale.

"No!" Jean cried. She turned to Drake. "Can Worm go after it? We must get it back!"

Drake shook his head. "Worm can only transport if he knows where he is going. There's no way to know where Maldred's orb went."

Jean sat down on a pile of silver coins. She put her face in her hands, but she did not cry. "I have failed," she said. "I am the first Dragon Master to lose the Silver Key."

Diego put a hand on her shoulder. "You are also the first guardian of the key to face Maldred. He is the strongest dark wizard the world has ever seen. You did your best."

"You did not fail, Jean. You were so brave," Drake said. "One of the bravest Dragon Masters I have ever seen!"

Bo nodded. "Drake is right. You did everything you could to protect the key."

"My best was not good enough," Jean said. "I am not worthy to be Argent's Dragon Master."

Argent began to shine softly. He nudged Jean with his head. Her Dragon Stone began to glow, and she gave a small smile.

"Thank you, Argent," she said. She turned to the others. "Argent says that he and I must not give up. He says we must search for the Silver Key."

"You can come with us!" Drake said. "We will find Maldred – and the key."

Jean shook her head. "Argent and I cannot leave this castle without permission. I will send a message to our king right away. As soon as I hear from him, I will join you."

"Good," Drake said. "We'll need your help."

Jean nodded. "I will be with you soon," she said. She stood up. "Before you go, I have something for each of you, Drake and Bo."

She climbed the treasure pile and picked up a shiny silver shield.

She gave the shield to Bo. "This is for you, Bo, for bravely protecting your friend."

Bo's eyes widened as he took the shield. "Thank you," he said.

Then she picked up a shiny silver sword and held it out to Drake. "And this is for you, Drake."

A MAGICAL PROBLEM

Drake stared at the silver sword. "Thank you for this gift, Jean. But I'm from a family of onion farmers," he said. "Farmers don't use swords."

"You have the heart of a champion – one who fights for a good cause," Jean said. "And every champion needs a sword!"

Drake took the sword from her. "Thanks," he said. "But next time I see you, you'll have to give me sword-fighting lessons."

Jean smiled at him.

"We must get Carlos and head to Bracken right away," Diego said. "We need to let Griffith know what has happened."

"Yes," Drake replied. "Let's go to the tower." Diego touched Worm, and so did Drake and Bo. Then Bo touched Shu.

Jean's Dragon Stone glowed again.

"Argent says thank you for your help," Jean said.

Then Worm glowed green.

"We'll see you soon," Drake told Jean. "We will defeat Maldred together!"

In a flash, they appeared on top of the tower.

Drake gasped. "Carlos!" he cried.

Carlos and Lalo floated in the air, inside a bubble of red magic.

"I'll fix this," Diego offered. He pointed his finger at the bubble. "Spell, reverse!"

Nothing happened. Diego sighed.

"Oh no!" Drake said. "What happened to your magic?"

"I must need time to recover from Maldred's spell," the wizard said.

"Shu, can you help?" Bo asked his dragon.

The Water Dragon nodded. She sent out another blue cloud, and the watery mist rained down on the red bubble. Carlos and Lalo gently floated down as the bubble slowly dissolved.

Carlos ran toward Diego.

"Diego! You're all right!" he cried.

"Yes," the wizard replied. "And I'm glad you are safe now, too. I'm sorry I used my magic against you."

"It's okay," Carlos said. "I know Maldred was making you do it."

"Let's get back to Bracken," Drake said. "Everyone touch Worm."

"Excellent!" Diego said. "I need to see Griffith. I think I know where we can find Maldred!"

THE GOLD KEY

Worm transported them all back to the Training Room in King Roland's castle. Rori, Ana, and Petra came running in, followed by Griffith.

"Diego! You are cured!" Griffith said, giving him a hug. "Excellent work, Dragon Masters."

Drake frowned. "Well, we saved Diego, but Maldred still got the Silver Key," he said, and then he explained everything that had happened.

"Maldred is so sneaky!" Petra said angrily.

"Yes," Rori agreed. "But I hope we get to meet Jean soon. She sounds awesome."

"She is," Bo said.

Griffith stroked his long, white beard. "It is more urgent than ever that we find Maldred," he said. "But I don't know how to find him. His magic lets him hide from my gazing ball. And I don't know the location of the Gold Key."

Diego grinned. "I know where it is!" he said. "When Maldred had me under his control, I could connect to his thoughts . . . And now it seems I can remember some of them. The Gold Key is hidden on the Island of Suvarna."

"I have a map!" Griffith said.

The wizard hurried into the classroom and returned with a map of Suvarna.

Diego pointed to a mountain on the map.

"The key is hidden inside a lair on this mountain," he explained. "Maldred is already on his way there, so you must hurry. The Gold Dragon and her Dragon Master will need your help."

"Thank you, my friend," Griffith said. "Now you need to rest."

"Yes, I would not be much help to you without my magic. I will return home with Carlos and Lalo," Diego replied. "You and your Dragon Masters must lead the charge to stop Maldred from getting the Gold Key."

Griffith turned to Drake. "Are you ready to leave for Suvarna?"

Am I ready? Drake wondered. *Maldred is more powerful than ever. How are Worm and I supposed to stop him? What if we can't stop him?*

He looked around the room. The other Dragon Masters were strong. He wouldn't be going alone.

Then he looked at the silver sword in his hand.

You have the heart of a champion, Jean had told him.

Drake took a deep breath. "I'm ready," he said. "Together, we will stop Maldred!"